# George

## Jules Feiffer

Michael di Capua Books • HarperCollins Publishers

To Madeline

Text and pictures copyright © 1999 by Jules Feiffer

All rights reserved

Library of Congress catalog card number:  98-74468

Designed by Steve Scott

Made in China

For information address HarperCollins Children's Books, a division of HarperCollins Publishers,

10 East 53rd Street, New York, NY 10022

First edition, 1999

13 14 LEO 40 39 38 37 36

George's mother said:

"Bark, George."

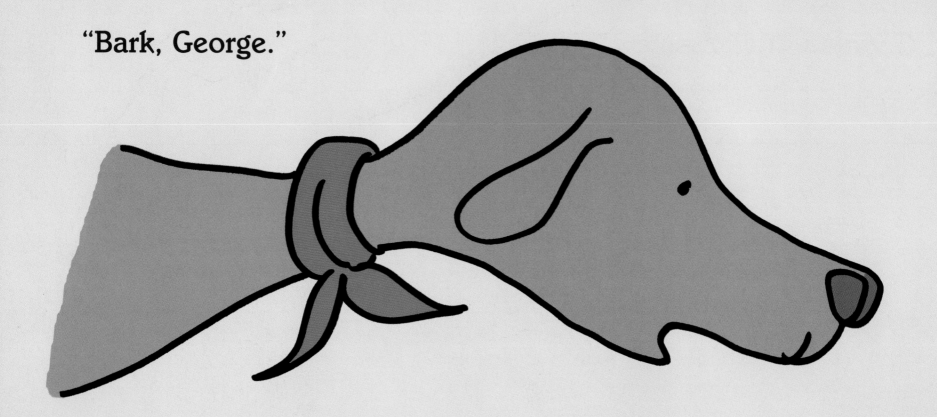

George went: "Meow."

"No, George," said George's mother.
"Cats go meow. Dogs go arf.
Now, bark, George."

George went: "Quack-quack."

"No, George," said George's mother.
"Ducks go quack-quack. Dogs go arf.
Now, bark, George."

George went: "Oink."

"No, George," said George's mother.
"Pigs go oink. Dogs go arf.
Now, bark, George."

George went: "Moo."

George's mother took George to the vet.

"I'll soon get to the bottom of this," said the vet.

"Please bark, George."

George went: "Meow."

The vet reached deep down inside of George . . .

And pulled out a cat.

"Bark again, George." George went: "Quack-quack."
The vet reached deep, deep down inside of George . . .

And pulled out a duck.

"Bark again, George." George went: "Oink."
The vet reached deep, deep, deep down inside of George . . .

And pulled out a pig.

"Bark again, George." George went: "Moo."
The vet put on his longest latex glove . . .

Then he reached deep, deep, deep, deep, deep, deep, deep, deep, deep, deep, deep down inside of George . . .

And pulled out a cow.

"Bark again, George."

George went:

arf

George's mother was so thrilled that she kissed the vet . . .

And the cat. And the duck. And the pig. And the cow.

On the way home, she wanted to show George off
to everyone on the street. So she said, "Bark, George."

And George went:

Hello